SUGAR HILL

HARLEM'S HISTORIC NEIGHBORHOOD

CAROLE BOSTON WEATHERFORD

ILLUSTRATIONS BY
R. GREGORY CHRISTIE

In memory of the Harlem Renaissance poets whose words still inspire.—G.B.W.

To Gabriella Christie follow your dreams.—R.G.C.

Library of Congress Cataloging-in-Publication Data is on file with the publisher.

Text copyright © 2014 by Carole Boston Weatherford
Illustrations copyright © 2014 by R. Gregory Christie
Published in 2014 by Albert Whitman & Company
ISBN 978-0-8075-7650-2
Printed in China.
10 9 8 7 6 5 4 3 2 1 BP 18 17 16 15 14 13

The design is by Nick Tiemersma.

For more information about Albert Whitman & Company,
visit our web site at www.albertwhitman.com.

SUGAR HILL, SUGAR HILL WHERE LIFE IS SWEET

And the "A" TRAIN stops for the black elite.

Where **APARTMENTS** are the height of style

and watchful **eyes** train every child.

Where the BEST and
BRIGHTEST
strive and shine

and
STAIRWAYS
lead
right to
cloud nine.

Where grand
TOWNHOMES
lend river views

and parties swing to
JAZZ and BLUES.

SUGAR HILL, SUGAR HILL WHERE LIFE IS SWEET

And the NEIGHBORS smile at all they greet.

Where DOCTORS and LAWYERS live next door

to the
OWNERS
of a corner

store.

Where

CHURCHES

offer music schools

that polish rough

stones into

JEWELS.

Where
DUKE
and
COUNT
plunk out
new tunes

and
ZORA
spins stories
by the moon.

SUGAR HILL, SUGAR HILL WHERE LIFE IS SWEET

And the
NiCHOLAS
BROTHERS
rest their feet.

Where **AARON DOUGLAS** births black art

and a young

FAITH
RINGGOLD

gets her start.

Where TALENT blooms in pageants, choirs;

and

prized

BOOKS

fuel

creative

fires.

Where

ROBESON

puts down

roots a while

and
SONNY ROLLiNS
hangs with
miLes.

And kids play  STiCKBALL in the street.

Where **Du BOiS** outlines social tracts

and

THURGOOD MARSHALL

plots legal attacks.

Where lovely

LENA

takes
Sunday strolls
that shoot
racist notions
full of holes.

Where
GROWN-UPS
lift the young ones
HiGH

and give them

wings

to touch the sky

sky.

SUGAR HILL, SUGAR HILL WHERE LIFE'S SO SWEET that PRIDE rings out on every street.

AUTHOR'S NOTE

Sugar Hill is a historic neighborhood in New York City's Harlem district. Harlem was for years a first home for European immigrants. During the Great Migration of the early twentieth century, African Americans—many the descendants of slaves—flocked there from the rural South. Harlem soon became a center of black culture, politics, and thought. Successful African Americans first called Sugar Hill home during the Harlem Renaissance. That cultural movement of the 1920s and 1930s saw African American arts flower and gain wider attention. Artists, writers, performers, and intellectuals explored their own culture and affirmed black pride.

Several leading lights of the Harlem Renaissance lived alongside African American professionals, businesspeople, and celebrities in Sugar Hill. Among the neighborhood's residents were jazz greats Duke Ellington and Count Basie; artist Aaron Douglas; entertainers Lena Horne and Paul Robeson; writer and folklorist Zora Neale Hurston; civil rights leader W. E. B. Du Bois; and civil rights lawyer Thurgood Marshall. As a beacon of accomplishment, Sugar Hill challenged racist notions that African Americans were inferior.

Children raised in Sugar Hill not only crossed paths with extraordinary role models but also experienced books, art, and culture at home and in the community. Music lessons and art and dance classes expanded youths' horizons beyond the narrow limits of segregation. Churches formed choirs named after African American composers and held pageants that nurtured children's talents. The children of the Sugar Hill neighborhood were encouraged to dream big. Artist Faith Ringgold and jazz saxophonist Sonny Rollins—both products of Sugar Hill—went on to do great things. The National Register of Historic Places lists Sugar Hill as a historic district.

SUGAR HILL'S WHO'S WHO

EDWARD "DUKE" ELLINGTON (1899–1974) was a pioneering jazz musician and band leader and one of the most prolific American composers of the twentieth century. Born in Washington, DC, he began playing piano at age seven, wrote his first song at fifteen, and arrived in Harlem in the 1920s. In 1927, he became band leader at the famed Cotton Club, a Harlem nightclub that had white patrons and black performers. Ellington referenced Sugar Hill in the song "Take the 'A' Train," which he composed with Billy Strayhorn.

WILLIAM "COUNT" BASIE (1904–1984) was a leading jazz pianist, organist, band leader, and composer. A giant of the swing era of jazz, Basie was born in Red Bank, New Jersey. He learned piano from his mother and began performing at parties and resorts as a teen. He also played at a theater to accompany silent movies. He arrived in Harlem in 1924, where his musical career gained momentum. Basie's early hit, "Jumpin' at the Woodside," refers to the Harlem hotel where his band rehearsed.

ZORA NEALE HURSTON (1891–1960) was a novelist, folklorist, and anthropologist. Raised in Eatonville, Florida, the nation's first black incorporated town, Hurston came to Harlem in the 1920s to study anthropology at Columbia University's Barnard College. She blended folklore with literature in stories inspired by everyday black life. Her books include Mules and Men, which explored voodoo practices, the novel *Their Eyes Watching God*, and her autobiography *Dust Tracks on a Road*.

THE NICHOLAS BROTHERS were a dancing team featuring siblings Fayard (1914–2006) and Harold (1921–2000). They grew up in Philadelphia, Pennsylvania, and on the Vaudeville circuit, which they toured with their own band. With acrobatic moves, the young Nicholas Brothers starred at Harlem's Cotton Club. Their most spectacular routine—leaps and splits down staircases—appears in the all-black film, Stormy Weather. They later taught many younger dancers, including Michael Jackson.

AARON DOUGLAS (1898–1979), studied art at the University of Nebraska and taught in Kansas City before heading to New York City to earn a master's degree at Columbia University. Douglas found inspiration in African art and was the first president of the Harlem Artists Guild. He contributed illustrations to such journals as the National Urban League's Opportunity and the NAACP's Crisis. He later founded the art department at Fisk University in Nashville, Tennessee.

FAITH RINGGOLD (1930–), a painter, quilter, author, and retired college professor, was raised in Sugar Hill. She created her earliest paintings at an easel that her father, a sanitation truck driver, salvaged from the trash. Her mother, a fashion designer, taught her to sew and to create with fabric. Ringgold is best known for mixed media works that combine painting, quilting, and storytelling. She is the author of more than a dozen children's books, including the award-winning Tar Beach, which is illustrated with story quilts inspired by her childhood.

PAUL ROBESON (1898–1976), an actor, singer, and human rights activist, loved acting and singing as a child. Born in Princeton, New Jersey, he lettered in four sports in college and played professional football before earning a law degree from Columbia University. After racism turned him off to the legal profession, he acted in plays with Harlem theater companies. Robeson starred in Broadway plays and in films such as The Emperor Jones. Best-known for singing African American spirituals, he toured the world as a concert artist and performed in twenty-five different languages.

THEODORE WALTER "SONNY" ROLLINS (1930–), a saxophonist who composed several jazz classics and received a National Medal of the Arts, was born in New York City. He grew up in Sugar Hill with musical peers Jackie McLean, Art Taylor, and Kenny Drew—and near his idol, jazz great Coleman Hawkins. Rollins first played piano but switched to saxophone as a teen and played at high school dances before joining the emerging bebop movement. He is known as the "Saxophone Colossus."

MILES DAVIS (1926–1991), a jazz trumpeter, band leader, and composer, was one of the most innovative musicians of the twentieth century. Raised in East St. Louis, Illinois, he moved to New York City in 1944 to study at the Juilliard School of Music. He was friends with saxophonist Sonny Rollins and hung with Rollins's Sugar Hill crowd. With various band members, Davis created bebop, cool jazz, and jazz fusion—styles of modern jazz. He is also in the Rock and Roll Hall of Fame.

W.E.B. (WILLIAM EDWARD BURGHARDT) DU BOIS (1868–1963) was a scholar, writer, and civil rights activist. He cofounded the National Association for the Advancement of Colored People (NAACP), America's largest and oldest civil rights organization. From the group's New York headquarters, he edited the Crisis magazine. The first African American to earn a doctorate degree in history from Harvard University, Du Bois wrote seventeen books, including The Souls of Black Folk.

THURGOOD MARSHALL (1908–1993), the first African American justice on the United States Supreme Court, was born in Baltimore, Maryland. A graduate of Howard University School of Law, he went to New York as lead attorney for the National Association for the Advancement of Colored People (NAACP). Marshall argued the 1954 landmark school desegregation case, Brown v. Board of Education. He served as U.S. Solicitor General before his appointment to the Supreme Court in 1967.

LENA HORNE (1917–2010), an entertainer and civil rights activist, was born in Brooklyn, New York, and began dancing in the chorus line at Harlem's Cotton Club at age sixteen. Known for her beauty, she sang at nightclubs before pursuing a movie career. Her film roles, usually musical numbers, were often edited out of films to avoid offending Southern white moviegoers. In the 1960s, Horne took time off from show business to work in the civil rights movement. She won a Tony Award for her one-woman Broadway show, Lena Horne: The Lady and Her Music.